"*Fauna Mae*

By Ni

MW00944827

Vienna,
you are
wonderfully
made ♥

Nicole
Perrine

Dedicated to:

Asa and Cynthia. May your ducks always be in a row and when they're not, that you'll be able to find the silver lining anyhow. Love you bunches.

And for Taren, who taught me how to *Keep Calm and Carry On,* even when it was the last thing I wanted to do. You're the best.

Table of Contents

CHAPTER ONE

"Bark! Bark! Bark! Woof! Woof! Bark! Grr!"

Eight-year-old Fauna Mae held a hand up to her mouth and giggled at her twin sister's antics. She pointed her finger at her pretend pet.

"Now, now, Fluffy." She spoke sternly. "You need to be a good doggo and I'll put this leash on you."

Flora-Fluffy stood up on her hind legs.

"Wait...you're not gonna tie that rope to *me*, are you?"

"Well..." Fauna answered, tossing her thick blonde ponytail over her shoulder. "*Maybe* not. But how can we pretend that you're my dog if you don't have a proper leash? *Everyone* knows that you have to have a leash if you want to be a good dog!"

Flora frowned.

"I know!" Fauna smiled. "You can hold onto the end of the jump rope with your mouth and then I won't have to tie it to you!"

"Okay!" agreed Flora. She put the plastic part of the jump rope in her mouth.

"Roof, Roof!"

"Oh dear, Fluffy has a cold!" Fauna exclaimed, putting

her hand to her forehead. "Time to take him to the vet!"

The two youngest Joy girls went into the living room where big sister Tansy had set up her all-purpose pet-vet shop, kitchen supply, and beauty salon. Tansy had set up a sign on the table next to the sofa that read "*Tansy's One-Stop-Pet-Vet-Wares-and-Hairs – Everything You Need In One Shop!*"

Zeb looked up and rolled his eyes from his perch on Mr. Joy's armchair. He was reading the latest edition of his favorite comic book *"The Incredible Beetle Boy!"*

"Oh dear!" Tansy exclaimed in a high and fancy voice. Her hands flew to her cheeks.

"Whatever seems to be the matter with poor, dear *Fluffykins*?"

Fauna giggled again then straightened up.

"I think he must have the *dreadful* doggo-woggo, Doc." Do you think you can save him?" She clasped her hands under her chin.

Doctor Tansy nodded solemnly, stroking her imaginary beard.

"Yes, I can see that. I think I have just the thing! Fluffy, get up!"

Flora-Fluffy jumped up into the swivel chair. She made her eyes big and looked at Tansy. Tansy leaned over to look into Flora-Fluffy's ear with her Dad's magnifying glass.

2

Slurp! Flora stood up and grinned from ear to ear.

"Eew! Gross! Flo-ra!" All three girls collapsed on the couch laughing. Tansy rubbed at her cheek where Flora had licked her.

Mrs. Joy walked into the room smiling at her three daughters. She had flour on her apron and was wiping her hands off on a dish towel.

"Playing *pets* again?" She raised an eyebrow.

The girls nodded, grinning. They had been pet-crazy since the beginning of November, when their neighbor's bulldogs had given life to *four* adorable puppies. They had begged and pleaded, but Mr. and Mrs. Joy still hadn't said if they could adopt one of the Granther puppies for their very own. It was looking more and more like the puppies would be sold and gone before the New Year.

"Okay, well I'll tell you what." Mrs. Joy continued. "Let's get our schoolwork out of the way while the bread is baking, and we'll see if we can't go next door and peek at the pups. I'm sure Mr. Granther would love some fresh baked treats and maybe a break from things."

The girls squealed with delight and gathered their books from the low shelf in the dining room. Zeb lumbered over with his nose in his comic book.

"Today we're going to work on a new project." Said

3

Mrs.Joy. "Thanksgiving is *only one* week away and we have something very exciting happening. Each of you will be working on creating a report and having a presentation."

The Joy kids looked around at one another in surprise. This was *new*. They knew a *report* meant that they would have to learn facts about something. A *presentation* meant that they would have to share what they learned with others. But they had never had the chance to do one of their very own before.

Flora was excited. She loved the idea of being able to share the things she had learned with others. She bounced in her chair a little bit.

"Mom?" Flora asked.

"Yes?" Mom answered.

"What kinds of things do we have to report on? Will it be like when we studied George Washington?"

"A little." Mrs. Joy replied. "All the kids at *Redeeming Grace Church* are going to do a little report, and the topic can be on anything you want. The only rules are that you need to have some kind of presentation and we need to have everything ready for Thanksgiving Day when we have our annual Thanksgiving Brunch.

The Joy kids were shocked.

"Anything?" Zeb asked. "Even if I wanted to do a report on *"The Incredible Beetle Boy"*?

The Joy girls looked at Mrs. Joy expectantly. Surely, they wouldn't be allowed to choose *anything* to present.

Mrs. Joy grinned.

"*Anything.*" She replied.

CHAPTER TWO

The Joy kids worked hard that afternoon. They got all their math work done in record time and after working on their history and science skills, they practiced their handwriting by writing notes for Mrs. and Mr. Granther

Fauna missed seeing Mrs. Granther in her garden. She liked to be out working in the lilies and iris beds this time of year, making sure everything was ready for the springtime.   This year, however, Mrs. Granther wasn't in her garden. She was sick in her bed and had been for several weeks. There was no large straw hat peeking over the fence to look for, no sound of her gentle humming to be heard as the children played. There were no peppermints to be passed to the Joy kids when they skinned their knees.

Now, with Mrs. Granther stuck indoors, there was only Mr. Granther and the Granther's bulldog Dwight who came outside to play. Missy was the momma bulldog and for now all Missy wanted was to be inside with her puppies and Mrs. Granther.

The Joy kids had visited the week before and were

looking forward to seeing Mrs. Granther and the puppies again. The puppies were very small and snuggly and sweet, with the most adorable chubby folds and wrinkles all over their stout and short, wiggly bodies.

"Now remember," Mrs. Joy said, as she brushed the top of the *Challah* bread before placing it into the oven to rise. "You want to make sure and thank the Granthers for letting you visit and be sure to tell them that we're praying for Mrs. Granther to feel better soon."

Fauna nodded. She peeked over at her siblings. Tansy was writing her note with big loopy letters and Flora was doodling little pictures on her paper that looked suspiciously like fat little bulldogs ice skating. Zeb had already finished his work and was reading his comic book again.

She needed to finish her note. She tapped her pencil against her lips. What would the Granthers want to read about? She thought about asking about Mrs. Granther's garden beds but maybe Mrs. Granther would be sad to read about her garden since she had to stay in her bed so much. No, the garden wasn't quite right.

I know… I'll write about our new school project!

7

Fauna thought. That would be something that would be a good subject but nothing that Mrs. Granther could be sad about.

"We have a new school project coming up. She wrote. *We each get to pick a topic or a subject and do a presentation. It will be at our church on Thanksgiving Day. I sure hope you can come!"*

Fauna signed her name with a flourish. Now she would have to have a *very* special report. Mrs. Granther would be counting on her!

The bread was ready to bake in the oven. It smelled like cinnamon and apples. It was Mrs. Joy's favorite kind of bread, braided into an elegant fat braid and baked with a shiny crust.

Fauna hoped that Mrs. Joy had made more than one loaf. She went with her sisters to get dressed up and ready for their visit.

"What do you think you might do your report on?" Asked Fauna as she picked up her brush to comb out her thick blonde hair.

"I want to write about kids who do things on their own." Said Flora. "Like when we studied about the

Abernathy Brothers when they went to visit Teddy Roosevelt!"

"That was so cool!" Said Tansy. "Maybe you could bring one of the Franzoso's horses to church!"

"I don't know about that." Fauna said. "I can't imagine Pastor Jones would be happy about having a horse to Thanksgiving Brunch. Even if it was in the multi-purpose room.

Flora looked a bit sad at this and stopped combing her thin, silky-straight hair, but then immediately perked up.

"I can still do the report about the Abernathys! I'll just dress like one of the boys and have spurs and a cowboy hat. Maybe I can learn more about what they wore and talk about those things too." She pinned a sparkly bobby pin into her hair, making sure to get her long bangs out of her eyes.

"That sounds perfect." Said Fauna, as she put a silver hairband into her hair. "What about you Tans?"

"I'm thinking… it would be *really* cool to write about the different kinds of math books we know and how even if they're all different, how each one has something that's really fun about them." Tansy replied.

"You don't think that would be kind of.. *boring*?" Flora asked.

"No. I like math and science and Juniper and I were just talking about how they use a totally different math at Kindness Christian School than we use. It was *really* interesting to me. Besides, I don't think it matters if other people are interested. Mom didn't say anything about that."

"I think it might be a good topic, Tansy." Fauna said. "I wonder how you might do a presentation about it?"

"That's the easy part! I just have to bring in the different math books and let people see them. Easy-peasy, lemon-squeezy!" Tansy laughed as she put her thick curls up in a ponytail with her favorite hair clip. It had a horse on it standing on his hind legs.

"You guys have such great ideas." Said Fauna. "I wish I had a great idea. I want my presentation to be *perfect.*" She looked through the clips and pins on her Mom's display. "Something that is really, really special and exciting." Her eyes rested on a silver clip that had a centerpiece in the shape of a paw.

"I know!" Fauna nearly shouted. "I'll do a report about puppies! I bet Mr. and Mrs. Granther would let me come over and help take care of them if I ask nicely!"

Flora and Tansy looked at their sister in excitement.

Nobody spoke for a second.

"That." Tansy said, tossing her curly ponytail. "Is an *excellent* plan."

"Right!" Flora said. "Maybe, *maybe* if you write a good enough report... we could see if Mom and Dad would let us keep one of the Granther puppies for our *own!*"

CHAPTER THREE

It was Saturday. Each of the Joy kids spent the morning working on their special reports. They had only five days left to work and they needed to make sure everything was ready to go.

Tansy was working hard on learning about all the different kinds of math books that were available to kids. Once she had permission from her Mom she began her work on the computer. She spent the whole morning researching different *options* offered to people. It turned out that there were many ways to learn math and even different orders in how you went about learning math. Tansy had printed off so many pages that she was *sure* to have a report that was interesting.

Zeb was working on his project in the kitchen. He had asked Mr. Joy to pick up a big poster board that had two pieces that folded inward. Mr. Joy had called it a *science fair board.* Zeb had wanted to do his report on the science behind *The Incredible Beetle Boy* and both he and Mr. Joy had mapped out his plan that morning together, using Zeb's comic book collection and books

12

about *entomology*, which meant the study of bugs. Zeb and Mr. Joy were covered in glitter glue and markers and were talking about bugs and cutting out pieces of brightly-colored construction paper and bits of tin foil. The kitchen floor was messy, but the Joy men were having a blast.

Mrs. Joy had taken one look at the mess they created and promptly threw up her apron, laughing at Mr. Joy and Zeb and claiming that she would take today to focus on the family laundry while father and son took over her kitchen. Lunch would have to be pizza ordered in since there was no way she'd be able to cook under such conditions.

Mr. Joy and Zeb had looked bashful at this, but high fived at the mention of *pizza.*

Flora was working on her history presentation. She had pulled up the story of the Abernathy brothers and was hard at work looking for other mentions of kids doing amazing things. She had named her project *Independent Kids of America.* She was keeping most of her work a surprise, even from Mrs. Joy.

Fauna had written out everything she could find about

puppies from the library the day before. She had it ready to print in her best handwriting and then she had gotten special permission from her parents to go and spend time helping Mr. and Mrs. Granther on Saturday. She was so nervous she barely ate her breakfast. She just pushed her oatmeal around in circles.

She would be going over to the Granther's house for lunch and then she would spend the day figuring out the kinds of things that puppies needed to be healthy and strong. Fauna carefully packed a notebook, some pencils and pens, and a clipboard into her book bag. She made sure she had on her nice jeans and a sweater so that the pups' tiny claws didn't scratch her.

Lastly, she put her paw print clip into her hair. She was ready to go. She put her bookbag onto her back and asked Mrs. Joy if she could go over.

"Yes, I don't see why not." Said Mrs. Joy, as she folded some of Mr. Joy's sweaters. "Will you just take over some of the muffins from this morning when you go?"

Fauna nodded.

"Sure Mom."

"And when you go, please remember to be a blessing. Remember who you represent." Mrs. Joy continued. She gave Fauna a big hug. "Try to help Mr. and Mrs. Granther as much as you can."

Fauna hugged her mom back. It was fun to go visit the neighbors all by herself, but she was a little nervous. She was glad it was only for the afternoon.

"What if they eat something I don't like?" She asked.

"Then you'll be thankful for it." Replied Mrs. Joy. "You get what you get, and you're thankful for it."

"Right." Said Fauna. It was a standard saying in the Joy home, and although nobody would ever say that the Joys were picky eaters, each Joy family member had one or two foods that weren't their favorite. For instance, what if the Granthers served *prunes* and *liver* for lunch? Eew.

"Off you go!" Said Mrs. Joy. "They'll be expecting you."

Fauna went to get the basket of muffins, looked around at her family, working hard on their projects, and went out the front door. She closed the door, walked down the path to the end of the driveway, and let herself out of the little gate, making sure to close it all the way. Then she walked over to the house next door, making sure to close the Granther's gate behind her. She marched up to the Granther's front door and rang the old-fashioned metal doorbell that was on the doorpost.

"Yap! Yap! Yap! Yap!" She heard a commotion and a bunch of paws scraping and thudding across the floor. Mr. Granther opened the door. He had puppies barking and playing tug-of-war on his pantlegs. He looked very tired. His white hair stuck up everywhere.

"Hello Mr. Granther! It's me, Fauna, from next door." She gulped. Mr. Granther was a very quiet man with big bushy eyebrows and a piercing look. Mr. Joy always said that he had a twinkle in his eye that reminded him of the proverbial *cat that caught the canary*. I sure hope I'm not the canary… Fauna thought. *He's an awfully big cat…*

"Hello Miss." Mr. Granther said brusquely, shooing puppies away from the door. "Don't just stand there, you're letting the heat out. Come on in."

He opened the door to let Fauna in. Immediately, the puppies came over to sniff her. Their little bottoms were wiggling with happiness. She reached out to pet the pup nearest her and scratched it's ears.

"Hey! That's *not* food!" she exclaimed. She pulled her shoelace out of one of the puppy's mouths.

Another puppy decided to pull on her hair.

16

"Ouch!" She shouted. "Hey! Stop!"

Mr. Granther looked over at his young charge, his eyes sparkling. He reached into his pocket for a squeaky toy and squeaked it, just once.

All the puppies immediately stopped and sat down. They had all their eyes on Mr. Granther's hand with the squeaky toy in it.

One pup yapped, then growled.

Mr. Granther raised one bushy eyebrow and then tossed the toy down the hallway towards the bedrooms. The puppies all raced pell-mell-rumble-tumble down the hallway trying to get the squeaky toy first.

Fauna laughed at the puppies. Then she looked at the kitchen table. It was spread with a fancy white tablecloth and set for three with bowls of hot soup and fancy triangles of grilled cheese. She looked in surprise when she saw who was sitting up at the table.

"Mrs. Granther! You're up!"

Mrs. Granther nodded happily. She looked like she had more color in her face than the last time the Joys had visited.

"Are you feeling much better now?" Fauna asked.

"Yes, darling. The doctors have said I can leave the bed, and if I'm very well-behaved this week, that I might even be able to go to your special presentation. What do you think about that?" Mrs. Granther asked. She wore a heavy velvet dress that zipped up the middle, and slippers with little purple flowers on them.

Fauna smiled.

"Are you hungry child? We're having tomato soup and grilled cheese for lunch." Mrs. Granther asked.

"I'm very hungry!" Said Fauna. "I could eat a whole elephant!" Her tummy growled loudly as if to agree with her words.

Mr. and Mrs. Granther both chuckled and they all began to eat lunch.

CHAPTER FOUR

Fauna was so tired when she got home that night. She had spent the entire afternoon helping watch the pack of puppies with Mr. and Mrs. Granther. No wonder Mr. Granther was so tired!

Every single puppy had to be given a bottle since Missy wasn't able to feed the puppies on her own. Mr. Granther would make up a special puppy formula and then put half of the special milk into a bottle and the other half he would pour into a bowl with a little dog food. Then, Fauna would have to help the puppies eat and then she had to make sure they didn't have any food stuck in the folds of their skin, because it could irritate the puppies and cause a sore.

After the puppies were fed, they had to go outside to run and play and as Mr. Granther put it… they needed to learn to *go* outside- preferably *not* in Mrs. Granther's garden beds.

After the puppies *went,* it was Fauna's job to clean up anything stinky that the puppies left behind. Fauna did not love this part of the job, but Mr. and Mrs. Granther explained that it as important to keep their yard clean and that it helped the puppies stay healthy to have a place to go that was clean. Fauna thought about what it would be like to use a restroom that was icky and agreed that while the job was a stinky one, it was a pretty important job.

After the puppies went outside, it was time for their naps. They all snuggled together with Missy and Dwight in a dog pile on a special bed that Mrs. Granther had made for all the dogs. Once they had all fallen asleep in their warm and cozy puppy pile, Fauna tiptoed out of Mrs. Granther's bedroom to see what more she could do.

The next thing that had to be done was that the muddy paw prints had to be scrubbed off of the kitchen floor and the puppies water dish had to be refilled.

By the time it got dark, Flora was ready to drop. She thanked Mr. and Mrs. Granther for letting her come and help with the puppies and had gone home ready to eat dinner and no longer be in charge of something for a while. The puppies were so cute and cuddly, but they had been exhausting to help with all day. Fauna wasn't even sure how Mr. and Mrs. Granther were able to do anything besides be on puppy watch.

Dinner was set on the table. It looked like Mrs. Joy had whipped up a family favorite, *Heart-Attack-Soup*. It was a delicious soup made with cheese, bacon, broccoli, and noodles and perfect after a long day of hard work. It was called *Hear-Attack-Soup* because it had a lot of ingredients that were not so good to keep your heart healthy. But once in a while, when served with hot whole-wheat-rolls, and a big salad, it was a perfectly good dinner.

Mr. Joy said even oatmeal would kill you if you ate it often enough, and that the trick was to eat what you loved best in *moderation* (that means only taking a small portion at a time).

"Enough is as good as a feast." Exclaimed Mr. Joy as the Joy kids filed their soup bowls and sat waiting for their dad to give thanks for the meal.

The Joys dug into the delicious meal, chattering about their day.

"And then, the bombardier beetle?" Zeb was saying to Flora. "They have two dangerous chemicals in their stomachs that cause explosions!"

Flora looked a little green at this.

"Zeb, uh, can we *not* talk about body parts at the table?"

Zeb grinned and said nothing while he ate another bite of soup.

Flora gulped.

"Well you guys won't believe what I discovered today about how many *amazing* things kids used to do. You just won't believe it."

"Well, you could start by telling us." Dad said, drily.

"No! I want it to be a surprise." Flora said. "I wouldn't want to spoil it for you. You'll have to wait with everyone else!"

"Besides," Tansy piped in. "I need more help with my math presentation. Mom, do we know anyone who has a *Shanghai* math book? I can borrow a copy of the *Norman* book from Juniper, and we have *Life of Fran* and *Math Ewe Visualize.* I just really think we need that *Shanghai* math book to round it all out."

Mrs. Joy looked thoughtful.

"You know, I think I saw someone was selling a copy on *Faceplant* the other day. I'll check it out and see if it's still available. It won't hurt us to have a different style math book in our library in any case."

"Thanks Mom," Tansy said "You really are the best!"

"Fauna, you're awfully quiet tonight. How was puppy watch at the Granther's house?" asked Mr. Joy.

Fauna yawned.

"It was good, Dad. I'm so tired though! Four puppies really is a *lot* of work." She replied. "I'm not really sure what I want to do for the presentation. I can't really show people how to clean up after the dogs. Although… Mrs. Granther was telling me she might be well enough to go to the presentation at church on Thursday. I want it to be really special."

Mrs. Joy and Mr. Joy exchanged a smile.

"Maybe you can bring the puppies with you!" Zeb said.

"Wow! Do you really think so? That would be so fun!" Fauna said.

Mr. Joy looked thoughtful.

"We'll have to ask someone at the church if it's okay. *Normally*, it wouldn't be okay to bring an animal into the services, but since this is a special occasion, we can ask."

"Thanks Dad!" Fauna said, yawning a second time. She started to think of all the ways the four puppies could be presented as they all finished their dinner. Soon it was time for bed and they all went down for the night. Fauna was asleep before her head hit the pillow. She dreamed of puppies all night long.

CHAPTER FIVE

Sunday morning came and went. The Joys were on their way home from the church services and talking about the morning's events. Pastor Jones had made a special announcement about the Thanksgiving Day Brunch with special presentations from the children who attended *Redeeming Grace Church.*

"Oh, Fauna?" Dad said, as they drove through the town.

"Yes Dad?" Fauna replied.

"Pastor Jones said the puppies were fine to visit for your presentation. He wanted to be sure you know that if there's any kind of a mess that you took care of it."

"Oh." Fauna replied. "Well, they'll be with me, so I'll make sure they know the rules."

"Juniper said she's going to do a whole report on ice skating!" exclaimed Flora. "She is going to bring a signed picture of Surya Bonaly!"

"Uh…what?…planet Earth-to-Flora?" Tansy giggled. "What is a Surly Bonalee?"

"*Surya Bonaly.* She's a famous figure skater who did backflips when she did ice skating!" Flora said.

"Wow!" Fauna said, impressed. "That sounds

amazing!"

"We didn't have a lot of time to talk," said Flora. "But I think we're going to have a lot of kids with some *great* presentations. Only four more *wake-ups* until we're going to do them!"

Zeb spoke up from the back seat.

"Pastor Jones said it was four days away…Dad, why do we count *wake-ups*?"

"Well, it's because it's hard to count days sometimes. As a rule, we don't count the day we're currently *in*, but that isn't always the way things are counted, so we decided a long time ago to count how many times we will *wake up* before a special event or day happens. It makes things easier for everyone."

"Oh." Said Zeb. "Okay. But what if we take a nap? That counts as a wake up too, right?"

Dad chuckled.

"You got me there, son. Not every system is perfect. Fauna, have you thought about what you're going to *do* when you present the puppies?"

Fauna answered with a grin.

"Well the puppies are too little to do backflips on

the ice…but I thought we could put them into a wagon and dress them up and have like a parade…a puppy parade!"

"Wow!" Both Tansy and Flora said.

"So cool!" Tansy said.

"Awesome" said Flora. "Best idea ever!"

"You could dress them up like the *Incredible Beetle Boy!*" Zeb offered.

"I'm not really sure yet, guys. But I'll let you know." Fauna said. "I need it to be *perfect.* The Granthers are counting on me!"

"Just so you're not taking on too much, Sweetpea." Dad said. "It's okay if it's something smaller."

"No, I'm sure it will be great, Dad." Fauna said. "I just need to make sure and plan it really, really well."

"Alright." Mr. Joy said as he pulled onto the Joy's street.

The family got home, ate a quick lunch of beans, cornbread, and fried potatoes and then immediately did what Mom and Dad referred to as getting *flat.* Sundays were the one day a week when the whole family took time to slow down, and not do heavy workloads.

Sometimes, the kids played, or they might go do an activity as a whole family, but for the most part, once they had lunch, everyone found somewhere to rest, to get flat, and to relax. Mrs. Joy said it was hard to do but that it made the whole week work better.

Fauna decided she would go to her bed and start writing ideas for her report. As long as she was resting and quiet, Mom and Dad didn't really care what she did with her time. She sat on her bottom bunk and started writing.

"*Puppies need a lot of attention.*" She wrote. "*They are a lot like babies. They eat without thinking of whether the thing they eat is good or bad for them.*"

Fauna tapped her pen on her chin thoughtfully.

"*Meow?*" Sulky, the Joy's cat, padded into the room and jumped onto Fauna's bed and bumped his head up against Fauna's chin.

"Hey Sulky." Fauna said. She scratched his ears and he started purring loudly and leaning into Fauna's hand. He was technically the family cat but Fauna was the person in the house besides Dad who he liked best. Mom said it was because both Dad and Fauna were content and relaxed most of the time.

Flora continued writing.

"A cat, even a kitten, is independent and smart. Dogs need constant attention and lots of rules."

Flora put her pen down. Rules were really important. They kept everything organized and that usually meant that things would stay neat and tidy and perfect. She had better think up some good rules about her puppy parade if it was going to go well. She took out another sheet of paper.

1. All Puppies Must Stay In The Wagon.

2. All Puppies Must Stay Quiet During My Talk.

3. No People Food Should Be Given To Puppies.

4. All Puppies Must Keep Their Costumes On.

"There." She said out loud. Sulky looked up at her and meowed. "Now we just have to come up with costumes and a way to decorate the wagon for the puppies to ride in." Fauna continued. "Do *you* have any ideas, Sulky?"

Sulky looked back at his person and blinked.

"Yeah. Me either." Fauna said. "Flora? Are you awake yet?"

She thumped the bunk above her head with her hand. *Thump. Thump.*

"Anyone home?" She asked.

"Bojangles." Flora replied. The bed jiggled as she rolled over.

"Bo… what?" Fauna giggled. "Are you sleep talking again?"

Flora's head popped over the top of the bed. Her long, coppery-colored hair looked funny as she peeked over to look at her sister. She scrunched up her face.

"*Bojangles.*" That's the name of one of the puppies. We could do a pirate theme. Think about it! Her eyes got wider. What if we did the boy dogs as pirates and the girl dogs as princesses? Everyone *loves* a princess. *Now.* Let me sleep!"

"Thanks, Flora!" Fauna replied. She pulled out a third piece of paper and started writing another list. This was going to be *perfect.*

CHAPTER SIX

It was Tuesday. Flora had gotten up early, before the sun was up. She had combed out her long, blonde hair, made her bed, and brushed her teeth. She ate her bowl of oatmeal and read her English assignment while Mrs. Joy drank coffee and worked on her laptop at the other end of the dining room table.

By the time the other Joy children came to the table, Mrs. Joy had put her work away and was frying up eggs and sausage in the kitchen.

Mr. Joy came in with a smile and hugged Mrs. Joy.

"Hello favorite wife!" He sniffed the air appreciatively.

"You forgot *pretty, smart, and amazing.*" Mrs. Joy teased. "Not to mention I'm your *only* wife. Silly."

"Right!" Mr. Joy agreed, nodding. "Any chance I can have some of that good-smelling food? I'm starving!"

"Here's your food and some hot coffee to go with it." Mrs. Joy replied.

"Delicious." He said. He pecked a kiss on Mrs.

Joy's cheek.

"How's the puppy report going, Fauna Mae?"

"It's going." Fauna looked up at her dad. "Only, I need some help. Do you go to work today?"

Dad nodded between bites of egg and sausage.

"Yep. Only since it's the Tuesday before Thanksgiving, I get a half-holiday today. So I'll be home tonight."

Mr. Joy worked as an inspector at a local rail yard in the next town over. He usually had mornings at home, would work late into the night, and come home after the Joy kids went to bed. That meant that helping with special projects had to happen on his day off or in the early mornings.

"Why do you ask?" He continued. "Did you have something you needed me for?"

Fauna nodded.

"I need help with the wagon, Dad. It's old and needs some help and I want to decorate it for my presentation. I have a list of things that I want to do."

Dad took the list his youngest daughter handed him. He looked it over.

"I think we can manage this." He commented, sipping his coffee. "Dear? Have we thought about the Granthers this year?"

"The Granthers?" Tansy asked, looking up from her math book. She yawned loudly. "What about them?"

Flora and Zeb were eating their breakfast and reading but glanced up to hear their mother's reply.

"We plan to have them over, if Mrs. Granther is feeling well enough." Mrs. Joy answered. "It depends on how the brunch goes. Mr. Granther should be updating me today to let us know what the doctor says. Either way, we'll make sure they have a good Thanksgiving meal."

Fauna blinked. She had totally forgotten about Thanksgiving. It was probably her favorite holiday. Tansy liked Christmas best. Fauna liked New Year's. Zeb liked *any* holiday that had food. But Fauna loved Thanksgiving the most. It was when Mom made all of her very best foods and the whole house smelled amazing. The kids would usually decorate with paper chains and find little ways to show how thankful they were.

"Mom, have you decided what foods we get to help with?" Tansy piped up. "I want to do the gravy again.

33

You *know* that's my thing."

"I think that will work." Mrs. Joy said. "Do you want to help with the rolls too? They're pretty easy."

The rolls were easy because they were from a bag of frozen rolls. Mrs. Joy was perfectly capable of making rolls, but since there were so many other foods that she cooked during Thanksgiving, she said she didn't mind cheating a little.

"Yes!" Tansy grinned. She didn't mind helping a little, I mean, it wouldn't really be Thanksgiving without helping make the feast- but the less fussy the recipe, the happier she would be.

Fauna listened as the family talk turned to the different foods they would each help with and finished her math lesson. She helped clear the table and washed her hands and face.

"Dad, when will you be home later? Can we work on the wagon right away?" She asked.

"You betcha, Sweetpea." Dad said, planting a kiss on Fauna's forehead. "I'll be home right after dinner."

"Thanks Dad!" She replied. "You're the best dad

ever."

CHAPTER SEVEN

The wagon was nearly fixed. Just as he promised, Mr. Joy had come home early and helped work on the rickety old wagon in the garage.

First, Fauna and her dad screwed in the slats on the old wagon, making sure to sand any rough edges smooth. Then, they had painted it a bright sunshine yellow and attached a fashion doll in a blue *Cinderella* dress as the *figurehead* to the makeshift ship. (If you don't know, a *figurehead* is a decoration used on the *bow,* or the front of a sailing ship.) Traditionally, they were used as a luck piece or to represent an idea or emotion, like bravery or speed. Fauna hoped the fashion doll would help bring *luck* to her presentation.

She wrapped the sides of the wooden wagon with pieces of aluminum garland she found when she rummaged through the family Christmas ornaments.

"We'll want to have these things out at the end of the week anyhow." Mr. Joy had said, as he brushed cobwebs off the box. He blew some dust off the top and set the large box near the kitchen door.

Fauna lined the wagon with a soft fleece blanket. She stepped back to admire her work.

"It still doesn't look like I need it to." She complained. "What does it need"

"You need a sail, silly." Said Zeb. "That's what you need. Otherwise, it's just a tugboat with a doll on the front."

Fauna frowned. Where did she put the mast?

"Better go ask Mom what she might have that will work." Mr. Joy said. "Did you need something Z? Isn't it about time for your shower?"

"Yeah, I guess. Oh, right…Mom can't find the plunger." He started digging through a bin on the shelf next to Mr. Joy. "Hey! Look! It's my old tee-ball mitt!" He continued digging through the bins and finding odds and ends.

"Oh!" Fauna blushed. "I've got the plunger here." She held up the plunger, making sure to keep her hands well-away from the business end of the tool.

"Hmm." Mr. Joy frowned. "I don't think we should use the one we use at home. Those dogs won't be able to resist all the special smells that tool brings with it. And who knows how sick they could get from bathroom germs. Why don't you let me run up to the store and grab one special for you?"

Fauna ran up to her dad and hugged him.

"You really are the best." She grinned up at him.

"I know." He grinned. "I'm handsome too." He made a silly face.

"Ker-choo!" Zeb suddenly sneezed loudly, tripping over his feet and landing in the dress-up bin. He had a pink feather boa on his shoulder and an army hat over one eye. His face was covered in dust.

"Guess I'd better go see about that shower…" He replied.

"That's the truth." Mr. Joy said. "I'll just run up to the store and be right back, Sweetpea."

While Mr. Joy fired up the family van, Fauna helped her brother out of the bin. Then she started looking for things to help her presentation pop. After digging through ballerina tutus, banana suits, cat ears, long, glittery dresses, and old robes, she discovered her goal: a pirate hat, eye patch, and a *Jolly Roger* flag, complete with skull and crossbones. She shook it out and looked at it. It was the *perfect* size for the wagon.

She pulled out a few of the smaller ballerina tutus and shook the dust out. They tied with colorful ribbons in the back, making them just exactly right for the smaller girl puppies. While she waited for her dad to return, she started folding and organizing the dress-up bin. Every time she removed a piece of fabric, she would give it a good shake and then fold it neatly. She found an empty basket and stacked the smaller dress-up items inside. By the time Mr. Joy returned, the bin was much less jumbled and so much more enjoyable.

Mr. Joy pulled into the driveway with the family van and walked into the garage, one sack of groceries in one hand and a brand-new plunger in another. He brandished it like a sword.

"Avast ye matey!" He cried. "It's I, The Dread Pirate Handsome!"

"Dad! You are so goofy!" Fauna laughed. "…and handsome!"

"Why thank ye m'lady! Now! Take this stout and fine mast and use it well!" He said.

"Yes, sir!" Fauna saluted. She loved it when a plan

came together. She spent several more minutes getting

the whole wagon decorated and imagining how perfect

the whole presentation was going to be. She couldn't wait

until Thursday morning!

CHAPTER EIGHT

Wednesday morning was spent getting the house perfectly tidied for the coming holiday. The Joys did a spring cleaning every April before Easter, and every Thanksgiving they did a fall tidy. The whole family worked together dusting, sweeping, and shining the whole house from top to bottom.

Mr. Joy would take his sturdy shop vacuum and make sure that the ceilings were clear of any dust bunnies and the vents were tidy. Mrs. Joy would polish the kitchen cabinets with an organic orange peel cleaner and then wax them to make sure they shined.

The Joy kids used this day to make paper chains and made sure they went through their old toys and make room for the new things that would come along in the month of December.

Fauna loved this family tradition. She loved that everything was clean and shining and had it's very own place. (It was nice to know when you put something somewhere that you would always be able to find it right away and to know exactly where you put it when you needed it.) Plus it kept everything safe and sound, so that big brothers, for instance, didn't step on special things and smush them.

Actually, Fauna was so in love with having everything *just so* that she finished her work early and went to go and help Mrs. Joy in the kitchen. Mrs. Joy was working on getting the turkey ready for his big day.

She was singing as she buttered the whole bird and then stuffed a bunch of fresh sage, minced onions, and rosemary into the inside cavity (*cavity,* in this case, doesn't mean a tooth problem. In general, it means a hole. When a bird is made into food, they take the insides out and just the meat and bones is left. There is a hole or a cavity there where you can put in fresh herbs and spices to keep the meat tasting nice.)

Fauna walked into the kitchen and watched her mom for a few minutes. She waited for her mom to turn around before she spoke.

"Mom?" She asked.

"Yes?" Mrs. Joy answered.

"Do you think I could have another job? I'm done

42

with my tidying and I need something to do."

"Well… let me see. I think I've got just about everything covered here." Mrs. Joy replied. "Oh! I know, why don't you go over and pay a visit to the puppies? Tomorrow is a really big day! You'll want to practice. Be sure and send our love to the Granthers."

"That's a great plan!" Fauna agreed. She went to put on her coat and went next door.

"Yap! Yap! Yap! Yap! Yap!" the sound of little paws scraping the floor was heard as Fauna stood on the front step of the Granther's house. Eventually, Mrs. Granther opened the door.

"Hello Mrs. Granther!" Fauna grinned. "My mom said I might come over and help with the puppies. Is that okay?"

Mrs. Granther smiled.

"Now that's the best idea I've heard all day!" She replied. "I'm all behind in my work since my sickness and I can't seem to get anything done. And with tomorrow being Thanksgiving too!" She let Fauna in the house.

"Where's Mr. Granther?" Fauna asked, looking

around for the bushy-eyed man.

"Oh, him." Mrs. Granther tsked. "Truth be told, he's got a cold and I finally convinced him to go and have a little nap. You can hear him if you can get these pups to ever stop yipping."

She took a squeaky ball out of her pocket and the yipping puppies all sat as still as statues. She squeaked it once and a pup barked, then growled. She threw it down the hallway and off the puppies went to chase it. It was quiet.

"Oh." Fauna paused. "Wow. I can hear it! I thought that was a lawn mower!"

"Nope. Not a lawn mower." Mrs. Granther said. "He's just got a strong snore. Actually, he and Dwight are *both* snoring. I don't think I'd be able to sleep at night if it wasn't for those snores."

"Really?" Fauna wondered aloud. "Doesn't it keep you up?"

"Not anymore dear. Not at my age." Mrs. Granther said. "Now, tell me your plans for tomorrow morning."

Fauna brought out her lists and her backpack with the different costumes.

44

"We, that is, Flora and I." She began. "We thought we would give the puppies little nicknames and show them off in the wagon. We thought it would be fun to have a pirate and princess theme. What do you think?"

Mrs. Granther looked at the lists and the different outfits Fauna had brought. She looked at the girl in front of her. She grinned.

"I think it's a great plan! Tell me all about it!"

.

CHAPTER NINE

Fauna adjusted the collar on her white blouse carefully as she listened to her brother finish his talk about *The Incredible Beetle Boy.* Zeb had really outdone himself. He was just wrapping up as the people in the multi-purpose room clapped.

Tansy had already gone up. She was sitting in a chair with Mom and Dad and the other members of *Redeeming Grace Bible Church.* Fauna peeked at the wagon. The puppies were all piled in, snuggled together and one of the boy dogs, the one Fauna had called *Bojangles* was snoring a little. She grinned over at her twin sister.

"Flora? Are you feeling okay?" Fauna looked at her sister. She looked a little pale. Almost green.

Flora gulped. Then she ran for the bathroom.

"I think she's a little nervous." Juniper said. "I'm sure she'll be great."

"I hope so." Fauna said. It would be terrible to be sick over Thanksgiving. All that pie gone to waste!

Flora returned from the bathroom looking a little better.

"You've got this Florrie." Fauna said. "You're gonna be amazing."

Flora looked at her sister and smiled.

"I'm sure glad you're here."

"Showtime!" Zeb said. He walked up to his sisters. "Boy there's a lot of people out there! I think we must have half the town here."

"Don't remind us." Muttered Flora. "Well, I guess it's time to go. Wish me luck!"

The Joy sibs wished their sister luck. Once she was onstage, she pulled out a rope and an old pop gun. She talked about how the Abernathy brothers had gone to visit President Theodore Roosevelt when they were ages six and ten years old. How they went all the way from Oklahoma to New York on horses by themselves to get there. She talked about how kids now were less independent and couldn't even go play in their front yards without being told it was too dangerous.

"This kind of thinking is bad news." She finished. "We kids should be independent and strong and be able to be challenged sometimes. If we can learn to try to do new things and not be afraid of what might happen, then we might have a better world."

She ended her speech with a bow and a sharp whistle to call her imaginary horse. Everyone clapped and she bowed and came back to where Fauna was waiting.

"Wow! That was fun!" She said, eyes sparkling.

"You did so great!" Fauna said. "Wait. Where did Bojangles go?"

Sure enough, when she looked over, she was missing a puppy. The other three pups were awake now and sitting up in the wagon.

"Uh-oh." Said Flora. "You can't stop now to look, you're up next!"

"What am I gonna do?!" Fauna said. This was *not* the plan. The puppies had to follow the rules or everything would fall apart.

"You'd better go up there. Just act like you only have three puppies. Juniper and I will look for Bojangles."

"Okay." Fauna gulped. Her tummy felt like there were frogs jumping inside. She took a big breath and marched up to the center of the little platform.

"Hello." She said. "My name is Fauna Mae Joy. I am eight years old. I wanted to talk about puppies today." The crowd looked up at her expectantly. She smiled carefully at Mrs. Granther, who was sitting in the front row. Maybe she wouldn't notice that Bojangles was missing.

Fauna took another breath.

"Puppies are hard work. They take a lot of attention. These puppies are well behaved because they have a lot of good rules."

"The first rule with puppies is you should never…hey!" Fauna frowned. One of the girl puppies was pulling on her shoelace.

She removed the puppy from her shoelace and cleared her throat again. This time looking at the puppy who had caused the problem.

"*You* aren't supposed to eat shoelaces!" She said. The puppy barked. The crowd laughed. Fauna turned to put this puppy back into the wagon. One, two… where was the other one?

She looked into the crowd. There he was. What was he doing. Oh. No. He was making a *puddle* on Pastor Jones' shoe. Oh dear…*gulp…maybe he won't notice…*

Fauna made a fast decision. She needed to finish her presentation. Now that she was down to just two puppies she would be able to finish. Hopefully, Flora and Juniper would be able to find both Bojangles and the other boy pup.

So instead of losing another puppy, she'd pick up the two girl puppies. She did this and stuck one puppy under each arm.

"Ahem." She continued. Her eyes were very wide. "So puppies need to be fed, a lot, they need to have a lot of attention, and.."

At this, the two puppies started wiggling and barking and before Fauna knew what had happened the pups had scrambled down her best dress and were making for the door!

"Oh no!" she shouted. "Quick, get those puppies!"

Soon the whole audience was in an uproar. Everyone was trying to chase the puppies to try and catch them. Pastor Jones had discovered his very soggy shoe and was trying to chase the puppy who had left his mark there.

Flora and Juniper ran up to the platform.

"Fauna! Quick!"

Fauna hurried over to her friend and her sister.

"What? What now? Did you find Bojangles?"

Flora shook her head.

"We can't find him anywhere."

Suddenly, there was a big crash.

The whole room froze as Bojangles came out from behind an artificial tree. His legs were covered in Christmas lights and his snout had what looked like maple syrup all over it. He gave a big slobbery grin as he sat down on the platform.

Fauna forced a smile on her face as she turned back to the audience. A baby started crying. Fauna felt like joining in. Could today have possibly gone worse?

Someone handed up a squeaky toy to the baby.

Squeak.

Instantly, all four puppies were silent.

Fauna immediately remembered the ball.

"Quick!" She shouted. "Toss the toy to me!"

The toy, a little plastic building block, was tossed to Fauna who caught it with both hands. Instantly, all four puppies were surrounding her and yipping and yapping happily. She sat down and gave them all belly scratches.

"Pssst." It was Zeb. "You have to finish it!"

Fauna remembered her job. She squeaked the toy again. The dogs held still.

"Um. So that's the way puppies are. You need to

give them lots of rules. Thank you."

Mrs. Granther, sitting in the front row started laughing. She laughed so hard for so long, pretty soon the whole crowd was laughing. Even Pastor Jones with his very soggy shoe was laughing. It was so silly to think that all this fuss could be caused by four small puppies, but at least they were all safe and sound. Fauna was disappointed that everything wasn't how she planned it, but one look at Bojangles sticky face and she knew that it was really going to be okay.

CHAPTER TEN

"Make way for Tom the Turkey!" Dad said as he brought the huge bird out of the oven. It was golden and crispy on the outside. The whole house smelled wonderful.

Everyone was just sitting at the table for dinner. Mr. and Mrs. Granther were sitting next to Zeb, who was telling them all about *The Incredible Beetle Boy* and Tansy, Flora, and Fauna were talking about all the unexpected things that happened at the brunch earlier that day.

"It's really a good thing that you thought of that squeaky toy." Said Tansy. "Although I don't think Pastor Jones really cares about his shoe."

Fauna blushed.

"Yes, he told me not to worry about it. He said when he was a boy he had a dog just like Jerry. I think he made a friend." Mr. Granther said. "I think Pastor Jones and Jerry will be seeing a lot of each other soon."

"Really?!" Tansy asked. The girls looked at each other. It was sad to think that the puppies would be going to another home soon.

"Now, don't get sad ladies." Said Mrs. Joy. "I think

you'll find that Bojangles here will be just as good as Jerry when we bring him home to our house."

"Bojangles…our house?!" Fauna squeaked.

"Yes! Yes! Yes! Yes!" Flora and Tansy shouted.

"He can totally sleep on my bed." Said Zeb. "After all, I am the oldest. And I'm the only boy. Us men gotta stick together right Dad?"

"Sure thing, Son." Mr. Joy said.

Mrs. Joy brought the last of the plates of food to the table. It was so good to be home, to be together. Everyone looked around at one another with full hearts.

"Let's say grace. Then I want everyone to share something they're really thankful for." Said Mr. Joy.

The prayer was said, then each went around the table to share what he or she was most thankful for. Mr. Joy said he was most thankful for Mrs. Joy and for his kids. Mrs. Joy said she was thankful for good jobs and the warm and safe home they shared together. Mr. Granther said he was thankful for Mrs. Granther. Mrs. Granther said she was thankful for her garden and for neighbors.

Zeb shared that he was thankful for comic books.

Tansy shared that she was thankful for being able to do school at home. Flora was thankful that she lived in a place where she could do anything she wanted to. Finally since she was the youngest, it was Fauna's turn.

"I'm so thankful… for everything!" She said. "And I'm glad that everything doesn't have to be perfect all the time. Sometimes, when things aren't perfect, we have the most fun."

At that note everyone cheered and they all began to enjoy the feast together.

Author's Note

Fauna Mae & The Perfect Plan started off as a story that was meant to illustrate the need for grace – *especially* when things don't go as planned.

One of the hardest things for someone who likes to have everything *just so* is to accept and learn that when things aren't exactly as we expect, they aren't necessarily *a failure.*

We try to teach our kids that they should always do their best, but that if they fall short, it is also okay. Life isn't always about being perfect. Sometimes, it's more about the journey we experience rather than the end goal.

If you would like to know more about bulldog puppies, the author of this book strongly suggests the reader looks to local bully breed rescue organizations. And a good training program to keep the chaos at bay. Modern technology has afforded us many avenues to research the plethora of dog breeds that are out there, and although the writer of this book has never owned an English Bulldog, she's always had a fondness for the breed from afar.

If you're interested in the hair accessories described in *Fauna Mae & The Perfect Plan* you can find those, including the super-adorable paw print clip on the author's website, found here: www.lrose.biz/alabasterjar.

With regards,

Niccole Perrine, Author

Sign up for the Joy Series Newsletter here:

www.nperrine.com

Joy Series

Tansy Joy and Too Many Tangles

Flora Jean and The Money Mix-Up

Fauna Mae and The Perfect Plan

Coming Soon:

Juniper Jade & The Dreadful Dare

About The Author

Niccole Perrine was born in Upstate New York, and raised primarily in Southern California and Southcentral Alaska. She now lives in Southwest Idaho. She is the oldest sibling out of six children, and a wife and mother to five children, whom she educates at home. Her favorite past-times include reading, writing, thrift shopping, and playing tabletop games with her friends and family. She is the author of the bestselling book *"Tansy Joy & Too Many Tangles."**

**#1 Amazon Bestseller Children's Books about Horses, September 2019

About the Illustrator

Teagan Ferraby is a Painter, Illustrator, and Graphic Designer. She illustrates children's books and covers, specializes in sea life paintings and has been hired for commissioned artwork. She attends The Cleveland Institute of Art where she is working towards a BFA in Graphic Design. Teagan's inspiration comes mainly from her hobbies such as scuba diving, reading, and eco dyeing. Visit https://www.facebook.com/Teagansart and https://teagan-ferraby.jimdosite.com to explore her latest works of art

Made in the USA
Middletown, DE
01 October 2021